DISCARDED BY
SAYVILLE LIBRARY

TOYS
100 YEARS AGO

by Allison Lassieur

amicus readers

Say hello to amicus readers.

You'll find our helpful dog, Amicus, chasing a ball—to let you know the reading level of a book.

A
Learn to Read
Frequent repetition of sentence structures, high frequency words, and familiar topics provide ample support for brand new readers. Approximately 100 words.

 1
Read Independently
Repetition is mixed with varied sentence structures and 6 to 8 content words per book are introduced with photo label and picture glossary supports. Approximately 150 words.

 2
Read to Know More
These books feature a higher text load with additional nonfiction features such as more photos, time lines, and text divided into sections. Approximately 250 words.

Amicus Readers are published by **Amicus**
P.O. Box 1329, Mankato, Minnesota 56002
www.amicuspublishing.us

U.S. publication copyright © 2012 Amicus. International copyright reserved in all countries. No part of this book may be reproduced in any form without written permission from the publisher.

Printed in the United States of America at Corporate Graphics, in North Mankato, Minnesota.

Series Editor   Rebecca Glaser
Series Designer   Heather Dreisbach
Photo Researcher Heather Dreisbach

Library of Congress Cataloging-in-Publication Data
Lassieur, Allison.
Toys 100 years ago / by Allison Lassieur.
   p. cm. – (Amicus Readers. 100 years ago)
Includes index.
Summary: "Discusses popular turn-of-the-century toys and how toys in the early 1900s were different from toys sold today. Includes "What's Different?" photo quiz"–Provided by publisher.
ISBN 978-1-60753-166-1 (library binding)
1. Toys–History–Juvenile literature. I. Title.
GV1218.5.L37 2012
790.1'33–dc22
                                                                        2010049882

Photo Credits
Library of Congress, Prints & Photographs Division, National Child Labor Committee Collection, cover, 15; SSPL/Getty Images, title page; Minnesota Historical Society, 5; Desiree Mueller/Photolibrary, 6; Smithsonian Institution/Corbis, 8; Bob Thomas/Popperfoto/Contributor/Getty Images, 9; Library of Congress, Prints & Photographs Division, National Child Labor Committee Collection, 10; Photo courtesy of Crayola LLC and used with permission. © 2011 Crayola., 11; Walter Zerla/Photolibrary, 12, 22; Quim Llenas/Cover/Getty Images, 13; The Granger Collection, NYC, 14, 20m; Vintage Images/Getty Images, 16; Wisconsin Historical Society, 17-bottom; The Granger Collection, NYC, 18; Archive Photos/GettyImages, 19, 20b; DSGpro/iStockphoto, 20t; Richard Nelson I Dreamstime.com, 20b; José Carlos Pires Pereira/iStockphoto, 21t; Waltraud Ingerl/iStockphoto, 21c; Italianestro I Dreamstime.com, 21b; Creative Crop/Getty Images, 22-top

1024   3-2011
10 9 8 7 6 5 4 3 2 1

Table of Contents

Wooden Toys	4
Toys for Young Kids	8
Toys for Older Kids	12
Homemade Fun	18
Photo Glossary	20
What's Different?	22
Ideas for Parents and Teachers	23
Index and Web Sites	24

Wooden Toys

One hundred years ago, toys were not made of plastic. They did not have batteries. Kids played with wooden toys such as blocks, pull toys, and soldiers. They built towers, windmills, and other structures from Tinkertoys. Bigger toys, like wagons, were made of wood too.

Small children played with rocking horses. Rocking horses were made of wood. They had real horsehair manes and tails.

Toys for Young Kids

Teddy bears were new. They were named after President Teddy Roosevelt. Everyone wanted a teddy bear. The first teddy bears were stuffed with wood shavings.

Original Teddy Bear

Kids used crayons for art projects in school. But they were expensive. A company called Binney & Smith invented a less costly way to make crayons. The first box of Crayola crayons was sold in 1903. It cost five cents. Each box had eight colors.

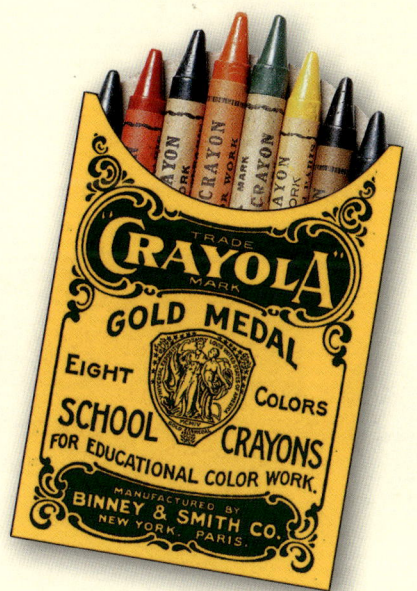

Toys for Older Kids

Older kids played with tin wind-up toys. Each toy had a key. Turning the key made the toy move. Animal wind-up toys turned flips, played musical instruments, or rolled across the floor.

Boys loved Erector sets. These building sets had tin strips and screws. Boys built models of bridges, skyscrapers, trucks, or airplanes. Some Erector sets were big enough to build Ferris wheels or robots. Some even came with motors.

SAYVILLE LIBRARY

Most girls played with dolls. Homemade rag dolls were made out of scrap fabric and yarn. Store-bought dolls had real human hair and clothes made of silk. Their shoes were made of real leather.

Homemade Fun

One hundred years ago, kids also made their own toys. Girls cut pictures from magazines to make paper dolls. Boys made model airplanes. Kids built swings from wood and rope. Everyone had fun.

Photo Glossary

battery—a small object that creates electricity

Erector set—a building kit toy that included strips of metal and screws to use for making models

model—a small representation of a large building or vehicle

plastic—a light, strong material that can be molded into different shapes such as toys

shavings—thin pieces of wood

tin—a soft metal that can be shaped into toys, cans, and other objects

What's Different?

These pictures show a toy car one hundred years ago and a toy car today. How do the toys look different? How are they the same?

Ideas for Parents and Teachers

100 Years Ago, an Amicus Readers Level 2 series, introduces children to everyday life around 100 years ago, in the early 1900s. The photo glossary reinforces new vocabulary, and the *What's Different?* activity allows students to compare and contrast the past and the present. Use the following strategies to help readers predict and comprehend the text.

Before Reading
- Ask children about toys they like and what they play with every day.
- Look at the cover photo. Ask students how they think toys from 100 years ago are different from the toys they play with today. Record their answers on the board.

Read the Book
- Read the book to the child, or have him or her read it independently.
- Point out details in the photos that are interesting or new to the child.
- Show the child how to interpret the photos and how the images relate to the text.

After Reading
- Ask the children to explain how toys one hundred years ago are different from or similar to toys today. Compare to the list they made before reading the book.
- Encourage the child to think further by asking questions such as, *What toys from the past do you think would be fun today?* and *What would be in your toy box if you lived 100 years ago?*

23

Index

blocks	4	robots	15
crayons	10, 11	rocking horses	7
dolls	17	soldiers	4
Erector sets	14, 15	swings	19
homemade toys	18, 19	teddy bears	8
model airplanes	14, 19	Tinkertoys	4
paper dolls	18	wagons	4
pull toys	4	wind-up toys	12
rag dolls	17	wooden toys	4, 7

The History of Crayola—Timeline
http://www.crayola.com/corporate/timeline.cfm?n_id=77

History of Toys and Games
http://www.ideafinder.com/history/category/toys.htm

Philadelphia Doll Museum
http://www.philadollmuseum.com

Stockyards Museum: Children of the Early 20th Century
http://www.stockyardsmuseum.org/index_files/Page732.htm